Welsh Folk Stories

First impression: 2011

Illustrations: Morgan Tomos

The original Welsh language series, *Chwedlau Chwim,* was supported by DCELLS.

ISBN: 978 1 84771 358 2

Printed and published in Wales
by Y Lolfa Cyf., Talybont, Ceredigion SY24 5HE
e-mail ylolfa@ylolfa.com
website www.ylolfa.com
phone (01970) 832 304
fax 832 782

Welsh Folk Stories

Meinir Wyn Edwards

Illustrated by Morgan Tomos

y Lolfa

CONTENTS

Twm Siôn Cati

It was market day, and the streets of Tregaron were bustling with activity. Twm Siôn Cati approached a crowd of people who had gathered outside the Town Hall, and he heard them whispering:

"He's a thief!"

"He killed a highwayman!"

"Nobody can catch him."

"The gallows will be waiting for him."

"But he's only helping the poor."

A man came out of the Town Hall, he demanded silence and then announced,

"In the name of Queen Mary, £10 will be awarded to any person who captures Twm Siôn Cati!"

Twm flitted slyly through the crowded streets like a shadow. Had anyone spotted him? He'd just arrived, but hadn't spoken to anyone. He disappeared through the crowd, jumped on his white horse and galloped away.

But before long, he heard horses galloping behind him, chasing him, closing in on him. He fired his pistol – one, two, three times. Some horses at the front of the pack fell, others were wounded or killed, and some of the riders decided that it was best for them to get away as quickly as possible.

Twm arrived at the river Tywi. He dismounted and climbed up Dinas mountain like a sleazy fox. The sunset was a burnt orange as Twm entered a cave, and he slept like a baby all night.

Twenty years earlier, in 1530, Twm had been born at Porth-y-Ffynnon, Tregaron, in the county of Ceredigion. He was baptized Thomas Jones – a very common name at the time. So he became known locally as Twm (Thomas), Siôn (Jones) Cati (Catherine, his mother's name).

Twm, his mother and his aunt lived on a little farm on the hillside, which was owned by the local squire. They worked hard but lived a contented life. Cati was only 14 years old when Twm was born and he often wondered about his father. He was never around and Twm would ask his mother about him from time to time.

Twm's father was Siôn ap Dafydd ap Madog ap Hywel Moethau, who had met Cati one day as she sat outside the house singing and spinning wool. He was soon smitten with her, and he bought the house from the squire and gave it to Cati. But Twm had never met him.

Twm was a mischievous child. Every day he would go out to play and would often return home covered in mud from head to toe. His favourite games were jumping in puddles and looking for fish in the pools and the rivers. Poor Cati had to swipe him clean with a broomstick!

Twm loved to play tricks on people. He was clever and could easily deceive his friends and family. Once, he gave Gweni Cadwgan a fright by wearing the horse's skull of a Mari Lwyd on his head. The Mari Lwyd was an old tradition in Wales, which welcomed in the new year.

"Help!" Gweni cried. "I've seen the ghost of a horse!"

During this time, Cati became friendly with Jac Sir Gâr and one evening, while Jac and Cati were sitting at the table, Twm tied Cati's skirt and Jac's coat together. When Cati stood up to fetch a spoon, her skirt ripped and that made a hole in Jac's coat! Jac wasn't pleased, to say the least!

A few months later, Jac and Cati got married and everyone sang and danced and composed poems for the happy couple.

"Watkin!" Twm said to his friend one evening. "Come on, Wat, I've got a plan!"

After dark, the two of them went to Tregaron, took down all the pub and shop signs and then hung them in different places, including the homes of a few of Tregaron's most important people. The Rev. Morgan Dafydd couldn't believe his eyes the following morning when he saw the 'Llew Du' (Black Lion) pub sign hanging in his front garden!

Twm got on some people's nerves. He could be very annoying, but others loved to hear about his mischief.

Y
LLEW
DU

Twm's relationship with Jac, his mother's husband, went from bad to worse. When Twm was 15 years old, Jac had had enough of his antics and sent him to work as a servant on Morus's farm, Cwm Du, on the other side of the mountain.

"It's time for you to grow up, boy!" Jac told him. "Hard work on the farm will do you good."

The servants had a tough time on Morus's farm. He was a hard master and they had to eat cold porridge for breakfast and watery *cawl* (broth) for supper. But one day, Twm had an idea when he smelled fresh bread coming from the kitchen.

"Siân, dear, can you come out here for a minute?" Twm said, imitating Morus's voice.

Siân ran out of the kitchen and Twm ran in! He grabbed a warm loaf, hid it under his jacket and ran all the way home to Porth-y-Ffynnon. When Morus found out that he'd been tricked, he promised himself that he would get his revenge on Twm one day.

Elias Richards was one of Tregaron's shopkeepers. He was a mean, grumpy old man and a drunk. He was Twm's next target.

"Good morning, Mr Richards," Twm said politely. "Do you sell large clay pots?"

"Yes, all sorts," he answered curtly.

"But these have holes in them," Twm complained.

"Holes? What do you mean, holes?" grunted Elias.

"Well, look!" Twm said, and he picked up a large clay pot and placed it over Elias's head!

"Ha! See! A hole large enough for your ugly head!" Twm laughed and ran away before Elias had time to take the pot off. He jumped on his horse and raced towards Llandovery.

Siop Elias

Twm loved to feel the wind in his face as he raced away from Tregaron. He stopped to let his horse graze in a field for a while and suddenly he heard a gunshot and a vicious voice shouting,

"Your money, madam, or a bullet through that pretty little heart!"

Twm spied on the scene from behind the hedge. A young lady fell from her horse in a faint, and the highwayman ransacked through her pockets and her bag. As he crouched on the ground, Twm went up behind him and struck him hard. The thief fell to the ground like a tree being felled by lightning.

The lady, who was called Joan, was very grateful to Twm for saving her life. She invited him to supper and Twm enjoyed a pleasant evening with Joan and her husband, Sir George, at their mansion, Ystrad Ffin.

Joan, Sir George and Twm became firm friends and some time later Sir George asked Twm to go on an important errand to London. He agreed to go, but he knew that he would miss Joan very much.

Twm set off on the dangerous and long journey, hiding Sir George's message in his pocket. Before leaving, he had filled up a small money-bag with shells and nails, just in case…

A few days later, just as he was getting close to London, a highwayman approached him, held a pistol to his head and begged for money. But Twm was prepared – he threw his "money-bag" into a nearby field and, while the greedy thief went to grab it, Twm aimed his pistol and fired. Then he jumped on his horse and cantered off. When he dared to look back, he saw that the thief was lifeless, and the road was covered in blood.

Twm realised that he was in big trouble. The authorities were looking for him. He had to escape.

He travelled from London to Geneva in Switzerland and lived a quiet life there for a number of years. When Elizabeth took over Queen Mary's reign, Twm was able to return home to Wales.

He went straight toYstrad Ffin to see Joan. Sir George had recently died and Twm and Joan were free to be together as a couple. Twm became a respectable member of the community, a judge and a poet. He had turned his back on tricks and mischief a long time ago.

Twm died in 1609 and the people of Tregaron, Ceredigion and Wales still remember his dramatic and dangerous adventures. Many stories have been written about him and read by children for hundreds of years.

Branwen and Bendigeidfran

Wales is the closest country across the sea from Ireland. The two countries have been on friendly terms for centuries but, once upon a time, things were rather frosty between the Welsh and the Irish.

In Harlech, north-west Wales, there lived a very important family. Llŷr was the name of the father and he had five children. The eldest was Bendigeidfran. He was a giant of a man, who became the King of Ynys y Cedyrn (the Island of the Mighty – the name for Britain at that time). His sister was called Branwen and there were three other brothers – Manawydan and the twins, Nisien and Efnisien.

Bendigeidfran was sitting on a rock one day, looking out to sea.

"What on earth…?" he thought. "Who's that? Is Matholwch on his way here?"

Matholwch was the King of Ireland, and thirteen of his ships were making their way towards the Welsh coast. The white silk sails were tied up to show that they were coming as friends, and by the time they got ashore, a crowd had gathered to give the Irish a warm welcome.

"Ah, Bendigeidfran!" Matholwch said. "Branwen has blossomed into a beautiful young lady. You know why I've come?"

"Yes, of course," Bendigeidfran replied. "We'll arrange the wedding at once!"

So, Matholwch and Branwen got married, as had been arranged, in a huge marquee in Aberffraw. There wasn't a building tall enough to accommodate the gigantic Bendigeidfran or large enough to hold all the guests. They had a lovely day – everyone, except Efnisien.

Efnisien, one of the twins, was a bitter and jealous man. He didn't like Branwen's new husband or the fact that he was taking her to Ireland. He slyly went over to the stables, where Matholwch's horses were kept.

"Ha! He'll be sorry he married our Branwen!" he mumbled to himself.

He got into the stables and, with a knife, he cut off the horses' ears, gouged out their eyes, slit their lips and chopped off their tails. When Bendigeidfran realised what Efnisien had done, he was mad with anger.

"I'm really sorry, Matholwch. I have to apologise for my brother's terrible behaviour. I'll pay you back for your loss, of course."

And to show that he had no bad feelings towards Matholwch, Bendigeidfran gave him some gifts before he left for Ireland – a silver stick, a golden plate, some horses and a special magic cauldron. Matholwch knew the magic of the Cauldron of Rebirth.

Branwen travelled to Ireland with her new husband, and she was treated like a queen. She received lots of gems and jewellery as presents. They lived in a grand castle and life was good. Within a year, she gave birth to a bouncing baby boy – Gwern.

But soon after, people somehow got to know about what Efnisien, their queen's brother, had done to Matholwch's horses. They laughed at the king, and he wasn't happy. He shouted at Branwen,

"Did you tell anybody about that? This is all your fault. You'll pay for this!"

And she did.

Branwen, Queen of Ireland, was locked in a tiny room in the castle. She was made to work like a slave and the king ordered the cook to give her a clout over the head once a day! She was a prisoner for three years. Her son, Gwern, was growing up without his mother. Branwen longed for Wales and her family back in Harlech.

"If only Bendigeidfran knew how Matholwch is treating me," she said quietly to the little bird who came to her window every day. She was convinced that the little starling understood every single word.

"Have you flown here over the sea from Wales? Do you know my brother, Bendigeidfran – the giant king?"

The only pleasure Branwen had during those dark days was speaking Welsh to the starling. It would sit on the window sill, bow its tiny head, listen to Branwen's crying and watch her draw an image of Bendigeidfran in the dust on the floor.

One day, she told the starling,

"I want you to do me a favour. Will you? I've written a letter. Here it is. Could you fly to Harlech and give this to Bendigeidfran?"

She tied the letter to its wing and, at once, the starling flew away across the sea.

When it arrived in Harlech, it could easily spot Bendigeidfran, standing much taller than everyone else around him. It landed on his broad shoulders, shook its wing and the letter fell onto Bendigeidfran's huge hand.

The Welsh king was furious, and he prepared for his journey to Ireland at once.

"Bring me the fastest ships and the strongest soldiers! We must save Branwen from the clutches of that brutal Irish king. Quickly!"

A huge fleet set off across the Irish Sea. In those days, the two countries were geographically much closer together than today. There wasn't as much water between them and it wasn't as deep. Bendigeidfran was able to stride easily across the waves. He was too big to travel on any ship anyway – it would be sure to sink!

Over in Ireland, Matholwch and his men could see the Welsh approaching, and they began to make plans.

"Ha! I knew this day would come," he said. "I'll never let the Welsh get the better of me again, oh no!"

By the time Bendigeidfran and his Welsh army had arrived on Irish soil, there was no sign of Matholwch and his men.

"Ha ha! The cowardly king has gone to hide!" Bendigeidfran gloated. "He's lost his bottle!"

But the Irish had destroyed every bridge to stop the Welsh from crossing the river Llinon.

"If he thinks he can stop me from getting to Branwen by destroying some pitiful bridges, he's making a huge mistake. Never! Come on men, cross the river by walking over my back," the giant said.

Bendigeidfran laid himself down, with his hands on one side of the river, his feet on the opposite bank, and all the soldiers walked over him to reach the other side!

When Matholwch saw this from his hiding place, he changed tactics. He began to flatter the Welsh king and apologise for treating Branwen so badly. She was released immediately and they held a sumptuous feast in a huge hall.

But Matholwch had secretly hidden a hundred men inside a hundred sacks, and had placed them behind the hundred stone pillars in the hall. Somehow, Efnisien got to hear about this and, while the feast was taking place, he slit each sack open and killed the hundred Irish soldiers, one by one! Then the battle began…!

Matholwch remembered about the Cauldron of Rebirth! He quickly placed the magic cauldron on the fire and threw his dead soldiers into it. By morning, the men had been brought back to life, but they were all mute. Efnisien decided that the best plan for him was to throw himself into the cauldron before the Irish could take their revenge on him. But the ancient magic cauldron smashed into four pieces and Efnisien died.

A much smaller band of men returned to Wales – only seven soldiers, Branwen and Bendigeidfran managed to make it back. The king had been badly stabbed in his foot by a poisonous spear and when he got to Anglesey it was so painful that he couldn't walk any further.

"Branwen," he said weakly, "don't be sad. After I die I want you to cut my head off. You must feast for seven years to celebrate my life and the birds of the goddess Rhiannon will sing the sweetest song every day."

Then, Bendigeidfran died. Branwen went to lie down by the river Alaw, while the seven soldiers continued their journey to Harlech to break the tragic news. Branwen thought about her dead brother and her son and the two countries which had been devastated because of her. She gave a deep, mournful sigh and died of a broken heart.

Seven years later, Bendigeidfran's head was carried to the Tower of London where it was placed, in his honour, on a pole, facing France. Even today, there are ravens flying near the tower to remind us of Bran-wen and Bendigeid-fran (brân/frân is the Welsh word for raven). They say that Bendigeidfran's head has saved Britain from invasion by other countries.

Branwen was buried on Anglesey, on the banks of the river Alaw. The stone remains of her grave can still be seen and people say that a starling is often to be found there, singing its sad song.

Macsen's Dream

Macsen, or Magnus Maximus (to give him his correct name), was born in Spain in the fourth century. He became an important man, who commanded and won many battles all over Europe. He was so powerful and well-respected that he was made Emperor of Rome.

One hot day, Macsen and 32 of his men went hunting. By midday it was too hot to hunt and Macsen decided to rest in some shade. The hunters laid their shields in a circle and made a shelter for Macsen from the burning sun. A golden shield was placed under his head as a pillow and, before long, he was fast asleep.

Macsen had the most fantastic dream.

In his dream, he climbed the highest mountain where he could touch the clouds. From the summit he could see many rivers snaking their way towards the sparkling sea in the distance.

He travelled along the longest river, walked through the greenest valley and reached the widest estuary.

There, at the seaside, he saw the most majestic city with a large castle reflected in the water. Banners flew from the high towers.

Macsen had a huge smile on his face as he slept!

He saw all kinds of ships floating on the waves. This was the largest fleet he had ever seen. One ship stood taller and grander than all the rest. It had sails of white silk and the hull was made of gold and silver.

Macsen walked along a bridge made of whale bones, which led to the ship. He then sailed across the sea to an island. The cliffs were rugged and the beaches were covered with golden sand.

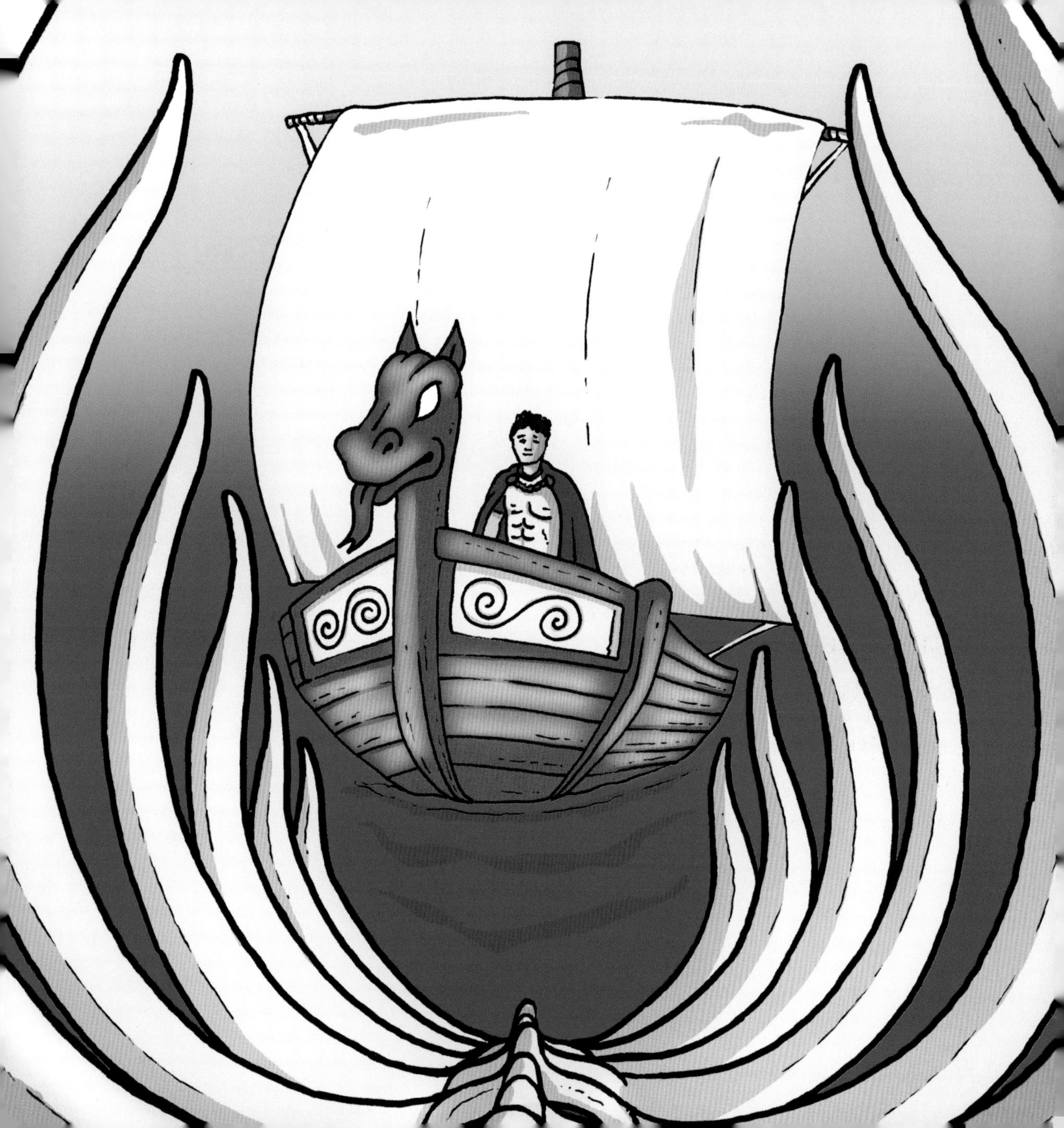

In his dream, Macsen travelled by ship around this magical place and arrived at a point where there was flat land on one side and a small island on the other.

There stood a huge stone castle on the flat land – the most beautiful he'd ever seen. He had to get off the ship and take a closer look.

The castle gate was open, as if to welcome Macsen and invite him inside! He walked into a long, vast hall which had a high ceiling and walls covered with precious gems and pearls. The doors were all made of pure gold.

Two young men were kneeling by a low table, playing chess with pieces made of carved gold. The men were dressed in black satin clothes, wore gold crowns and sandals made of the very best Spanish leather.

At the far end of the long, vast hall, an old man sat on a majestic ivory chair with carved eagles for its arms.

And then, Macsen saw the most beautiful girl in the world! She was incredibly pretty! The sun lit up her golden hair. She wore a long dress of white silk. The gold crown on her head was covered with gems and pearls, and she had a gold band around her tiny waist.

The girl ran towards Macsen, put her arms around his neck and then ... HE WOKE UP!

Macsen heard the dogs barking, the shields clashing, the hunting horns blaring and the horses neighing – and he felt both very happy and very sad.

He had fallen head over heels in love with the girl in his dream and he knew that he had to find her. He no longer wanted to feast or hunt or enjoy himself any more.

"I must go and look for her," he told his servants one day. "I can't live without her."

"But sir," one of his servants said, "people are making fun of you. They're losing patience and no longer respect you as their leader, sir. What are you going to do?"

Macsen ordered thirteen messengers to travel all over the world to search for the girl in his dreams. He described his dream to them in detail and two years later they returned with the mission accomplished!

Macsen felt happy for the first time in two years. His dream was turning into reality!

Leaving Rome, Macsen and his men climbed the high mountain and followed the wide river down to the sea. They went past the majestic city and the castle with high towers. Then they sailed on the ship with white silk sails across the sea until they reached Britain with the rugged cliffs and golden sand. They travelled around this island until they came to Anglesey on one side and Gwynedd on the other side.

And, exactly as in his dream, he saw the stone castle of Aber Saint with its gate wide open. Macsen walked through the gate, his heart beating like a drum!

In the long, vast hall with the high ceiling he saw the two young men, Cynan and Gadeon, playing chess. Their father, Eudaf, was sitting on the ivory chair, carving chess pieces from a large bar of gold.

And then Macsen saw her – the girl of his dreams, the most beautiful girl in the world – Elen!

"At last! Here you are!" Macsen said. "Will you marry me and make me the happiest man on earth?"

Elen ran towards him, put her arms around his neck and said, "Yes, of course!"

"You'll become the Empress of Rome," Macsen told her, excitedly. "I'll give you anything you want!"

Macsen had three castles built for his bride-to-be – in Caernarfon, Caerllion (Caerleon) and Caerfyrddin (Carmarthen) and a triangle of roads to connect the three. Some soil was transported from Rome to Caernarfon so that Macsen could feel at home there.

Elen and Macsen got married and Eudaf, Elen's father, received Britain as a gift from his son-in-law. Everyone was over the moon!

Seven years passed and the people of Rome, in Macsen's absence, chose a new Emperor. This new Emperor sent a short but nasty note to Macsen, threatening him,

"If you ever come back to Rome, I'll..."

And Macsen replied,

"If I ever come back to Rome, I'll..." and that was that!

And after many discussions, Macsen announced, "I have to go back to Rome to claim my Empire."

So Elen, Macsen and his army travelled to Rome, conquering France and part of Italy on their way. But what kind of welcome would he receive in Rome after seven years?

Rome was the only city left that Macsen hadn't conquered. His army just couldn't break through the city walls. They had tried for months and months.

One day, Elen saw an army approaching Rome. She ran to Macsen, smiling from ear to ear, and shouted,

"Macsen! Quick! Cynan and Gadeon have brought an army to help us enter the city!"

"Thank goodness for that!" said Macsen.

Cynan assessed the situation and then said wisely,

"The walls are the problem. We need ladders to climb up the walls. But let's wait until the Emperor and the Romans are eating lunch and then attack!"

And that's what they did!

The Emperor and his army were killed during their midday feast. They didn't have time to prepare to fight or to even wear their armour for protection. Macsen, Cynan and Gadeon's army had conquered Rome together.

Macsen and Elen got a warm welcome from the Romans. Macsen was made Emperor once again and he reclaimed his Empire.

Cynan decided to return to Wales and Gadeon lived in an area which is now called Brittany, in north-west France.

Macsen and Elen lived happily ever after. Macsen slept with a broad smile on his face every night. It just goes to show that, sometimes, dreams really can come true!

The Lady of the Lake

Hywel, a young shepherd, lived with his mother on Blaen Sawdde Farm, at the foot of the Black Mountain in Carmarthenshire. They lived a quiet and simple life following the tragedy of losing Hywel's father and two older brothers in battle.

Hywel roamed the mountain every day to care for his sheep and at midday he used to sit by the lake to eat the packed lunch that his mother had prepared for him.

The lake, called Llyn y Fan Fach, was set in a peaceful, lonely place on the mountain. Hywel loved to go there and watch the clouds reflected in the still water.

One beautiful summer day he went to sit on the grass by the lake as usual to eat his cheese sandwich.

"This is the life!" he thought, dreamily. "Relaxing by the lake on a sunny day…"

But, before he had taken the first bite of his sandwich, Hywel noticed something that would change his life for ever.

A young girl had appeared in the middle of the lake, right before his eyes – as if someone had lifted her by the soles of her feet and left her floating on the water!

As Hywel watched her, she began to comb her long blond hair with a golden comb, and gazed at her reflection. She knew that Hywel was watching her. She looked at him, gave him a broad smile and said in a quiet, shy voice,

"Hello, Hywel!"

"Who are you? Do I know you?" he asked in surprise.

"Can I have a bite of your bread?"

"Yes, of course you can," he answered.

He tore off a corner of his sandwich and gave it to the girl. She took a tiny bite and said,

"Ych! That's dry and too hard!"

She turned away and disappeared smoothly under the water.

Hywel raced home, his heart pounding in his chest.

Where on earth did she come from? How did she know my name? he wondered. As he ran in to the house, he shouted,

"Mam, I've seen a girl in the lake!"

"Hywel bach," his mother said, "calm down! Come and sit here for a minute."

And she told him the old story that had been told in the area for centuries about the rich, clever fairies who lived in the lake.

"But, Mam, I'm going back tomorrow to see her again!"

"Well, I can't stop you from doing that," his mother said, "but be careful, that's all I say."

After a sleepless night of tossing and turning, Hywel set off to work the following morning with a fresh loaf of bread in his bag.

Hywel couldn't wait for midday! He couldn't concentrate on his work at all, and he had a huge smile on his face all morning. When the sun was high in the sky, he raced down to the edge of the lake, he sat and waited. He waited until his smile started to fade. It got colder as the afternoon wore on and poor Hywel was just about to give up and go back to the farm for his tea, when he saw blond hair rising from the lake.

Hywel stood up and as he walked into the lake he said,

"Hello! I've brought you some fresh bread!"

"Thanks, Hywel, you are very kind."

She took a tiny bite and said,

"Ych! It's got too much yeast in it!"

And then, once again, she disappeared under the water.

Hywel walked home in a sulk. How could he make the lady of the lake like him? He decided to bake another loaf of bread and try his luck again the following day.

Lunchtime arrived, and he walked to the edge of the lake, longing for her to appear.

He waited and waited.

It began to get dark and Hywel had given up all hope of seeing her that day, when suddenly she appeared, in the gloomy dusk. He ran to her, gave her a piece of bread, and held his breath as she took a tiny bite.

"Mm, this is perfect! I'll be your wife if you're willing to marry me!" she said, and then she disappeared again! Well!

Suddenly, an old man with a long white beard appeared from under the water. There were three girls standing beside him.

"If you want to marry Nel," the old man told Hywel, "you'll have to work out which one she is."

Hywel couldn't believe it. The three ladies of the lake looked exactly the same, like identical triplets. Their hair, eyes, smile, height, dress – all exactly the same! Hywel stared at the three in turn and noticed that one of them moved her foot slightly. That was his sign!

"That one is Nel!" he shouted with excitement, pointing to the girl on the right.

"Correct!" said the old man. "You can marry Nel. My wedding gift to you will be some stock for your farm. But there is one condition. If you strike Nel three times, she will come back to the lake, bringing all the animals with her."

"That's no problem!" Hywel said. "Don't worry, I will never hit her."

So, Nel and Hywel got married. People came from all over the county to see the lady of the lake – the church was overflowing! They went to live together on a farm called Esgair Llaethdy, near the little village of Myddfai.

The years rolled by, they had three sons and life was good.

One day, they were getting ready to go to a christening at the church.

"Come on, Nel, hurry up!" Hywel told her. "It's quite a long walk and I don't want to be late."

"I know, I know. I'll just get my coat from upstairs."

"Well, get a move on!" Hywel said as he hit her lightly on the arm.

"Hywel, what have you done?" Nel cried. "Please don't hit me again, or you know what will happen…"

Another year passed and Hywel and Nel received an invitation to a wedding. On the wedding day they both got dressed in their best clothes and off they went to the ceremony. The church was adorned with spring's finest flowers and everybody was feeling happy. Everyone except Nel. During the ceremony, she began to cry her eyes out, making loud sobbing noises.

"Nel, what's the matter? Shhh!" Hywel said, and he tapped her arm gently.

"Oh, no!" cried Nel, making even more noise. "You've struck me twice! You must be very careful from now on!"

Hywel was devastated. He'd better not hit her again or he'd lose her. Forever.

Some time after the wedding fiasco, Nel and Hywel attended a funeral of a little old lady from the village. The church was full of people paying their respects. The atmosphere was sad and sombre. But suddenly, in the subdued silence, Nel burst out laughing!

"Nel, stop it! Shhh, don't laugh," Hywel whispered and he hit her softly with his glove.

"Oh, no!" Nel cried. "Hywel, you've hit me three times!" She ran out of the church, in front of a shocked congregation.

Nel ran to Esgair Llaethdy and called on all the cows and sheep and pigs and horses to follow her to the lake, where they all disappeared into the deep water.

Hywel broke his heart and he died soon after. The three sons would go to the lake every day, in the hope of seeing their mother once again.

And one day, she emerged from the water and came to stand by their side, with her hair dripping wet.

"My sons," she said gently. "I have an important message for you."

She gave each son a package of herbs and some books containing recipes and potions on how to cure people by using the herbs and plants which grew in the countryside all around them.

The sons became famous doctors. The Physicians of Myddfai (Meddygon Myddfai) could cure any illness and their recipes can still be read today in the *Red Book of Hergest (Llyfr Coch Hergest).*

If you venture near Llyn y Fan Fach for a picnic on a warm day, look carefully towards the middle of the lake, because you never know what could appear before your very eyes...

Rebecca's Daughters

"John, get up, quickly! There's a terrible noise coming from next door."

"What? From the tollhouse?"

"Yes, look, the tollhouse is on fire. There are people everywhere. I hope Sarah's alright."

Suddenly, there was a knock at the front door of John and Margaret Thomas's cottage and Sarah Williams rushed in. Her face was black with soot, and blood was pouring from an open wound on her head.

"Help me!" the old woman cried. "Or they'll take everything!"

"Who are 'they', Sarah?" Margaret asked.

"Rebecca's Daughters, of course. Half of my belongings are out on the road. Come with me, please!"

They managed to drag a few of her belongings back to the cottage but, by the following morning, Sarah was dead.

It was September 1843 and Sarah Williams was the latest victim of a gang who travelled all over west Wales to protest about tollgates being placed across the roads. They had to pay three pence to the tollkeeper to open the tollgate so that they could carry on with their journey to market or to town.

New roads were built all across south-west Wales and, although these roads made travelling by horse and cart much more comfortable, it was much more expensive to travel around.

The farmers were poor and had no money to pay the tolls. The harvest had failed for three years and they had to pay high rents to the wealthy landowners to live in their small cottages. They also had to pay tithes to the Church of England. This was so unfair, because ordinary Welsh people went to chapel on a Sunday and not to church like the rich.

Some farmers had to sell a pig, a sheep, or even a watch or a wedding ring in order to pay their debts. In those days, the only food available was bread, potatoes and milk. Meat was a rare treat but some were lucky enough to be able to make their own cheese. Times were really tough and some had had enough and decided that they had to protest.

Word spread that a meeting was to be held near Mynachlog-ddu, in the Preseli mountains of Pembrokeshire.

"Hey, Twm Carnabwth has arranged a meeting, you know..."

"... on Glynsaithmaen farm."

"He's thought of a fantastic idea!"

"Well, *I'll* definitely be there!"

Twm Carnabwth was a farmer in the area, and a well-known boxer. People respected him, and excitement was at fever pitch at the meeting.

"Friends," said Twm to the hundreds who had gathered there. "Another tollgate has been erected – at Efailwen this time, right across the road. We've got to destroy it. We have to stick together and protest against these tolls!"

Four hundred people gathered together on a dark night in Efailwen. They were a terrifying crowd – they had blackened faces and each carried an axe or a stick, a saw or a flaming torch. Their sharp weapons glistened in the light of the moon. Some had dressed in women's clothes and wore long wigs so that no-one could recognise them.

Hearing the horses' hooves and the clattering of wooden clogs getting nearer, Ned Owen, Efailwen's tollkeeper, stood shaking in his boots. He then ran out through the back door of the tollhouse before the gang could get to him.

Astride his large white stallion at the front of the crowd, Twm, or 'Becca' as he was known that night, gave the order to smash down the gate and burn the house to the ground.

That was just the beginning.

Rebecca, or Becca, and her followers became famous, but they were shrouded in mystery. Who were they? The authorities had no idea! Why did they dress up in women's clothes and blacken their faces? Why couldn't they be caught and punished?

There was no police force in Wales at this time. Punishment was given out by people in authority and most of them were rich and had come to live in Wales from England. One form of punishment was the wooden horse. This horse was carried from one place to another, and anyone caught stealing, fighting or committing some terrible crime would be put on the wooden horse in front of a crowd who would beat drums and shout insults. The criminals sitting on the wooden horse would sometimes wear women's clothes and blacken their faces so that they couldn't be identified. Rebecca's Daughters had followed this tradition.

It was a clear, moonlit February night in Whitland and the annual fair was in full swing. Inside the Golden Lion pub, a pig farmer claimed that Rebecca was about to attack.

He was right. The Trefechan tollgate nearby was destroyed that night. When the authorities went to the Golden Lion to question the drinkers, the pig farmer told them that he knew who two of Rebecca's Daughters were. The two were then caught and brought to court. But they were soon released, and the pig farmer was arrested for telling lies!

Rebecca's Daughters attacked at least once a week. All five Lampeter tollgates were destroyed during one night and Porth-y-rhyd's gate was smashed and rebuilt nine times within a couple of weeks!

By 1840, Rebecca's Daughters were famous. More and more Daughters joined the campaign throughout Wales – from Llandeilo to Llangurig, Llandysul to Llanelli. They were all very brave to fight for their rights as farmers. But there was one question on everyone's lips – who on earth was this 'Rebecca' behind the mayhem?

Well, Twm Carnabwth was the first Rebecca, back in Efailwen, but each area had its own Rebecca as a leader. There was Dai'r Cantwr, Shoni Sgubor Fawr and Jac Tŷ Isha, who lead attacks on tollhouses and tollgates. All of these men were tall and strong, and the tollkeepers and the constables, who had been sent to Wales from London, were scared stiff of them. Rebecca and her Daughters managed to escape every time.

In Llandysul, 600 people marched towards the tollgate, and the constables there ran for their lives!

In Llanfihangel-ar-Arth, Rebecca and her Daughters formed a circle around the constables and forced *them* to smash the gate with their truncheons!

In Pwll-trap, Rebecca's Daughters arrived at the tollhouse. Rebecca casually leaned on the gate and said in a lady's voice:

"Oh, dear me, girls. What have we got here? I can't walk another step!"

"Why, Mam?" the 'girls' shouted.

"Well!" Rebecca answered slowly and clearly. "There's a gate in my way and it is locked."

"We'll have to break it down, then!"

"Good, girls! All together!"

Ten minutes later, they were gone, leaving a terrible mess behind them.

But there was one important attack left…

… on the workhouse in Carmarthen, where farmers and their families were forced to live if they hadn't paid their debts.

All the shops were shut and the narrow streets were empty. The town was waiting for the attack.

At the nearby Plough and Harrow pub, 2,000 people gathered. There was a carnival atmosphere – the sun shone, a band played and everyone was in high spirits. They marched to Carmarthen and arrived at the workhouse. They were prepared to riot. Someone had got hold of the key, the front door was unlocked and all the workhouse poor ran out to freedom!

But things started to go wrong when a shout was heard:

"The soldiers are coming! They have horses and swords!"

Rebecca and her Daughters ran in a panic in all directions. Many were caught, some were imprisoned and some were exiled to live on the other side of the world.

That day in Carmarthen was the beginning of the end for Rebecca's Daughters. By 1843 there was a sense that the authorities were beginning to win the battle. More and more rioters were caught and many believed that the antics of Rebecca's Daughters had gone too far.

The *Times* newspaper in London published accounts of the riots and Queen Victoria came to learn about the plight of farmers in rural Wales. She commissioned a detailed report into how their standard of living could be improved and how to regulate the tolls more fairly. All they had wanted was fair play. So, Rebecca's Daughters had achieved what they set out to do in the first place.

Other books published by Y Lolfa:

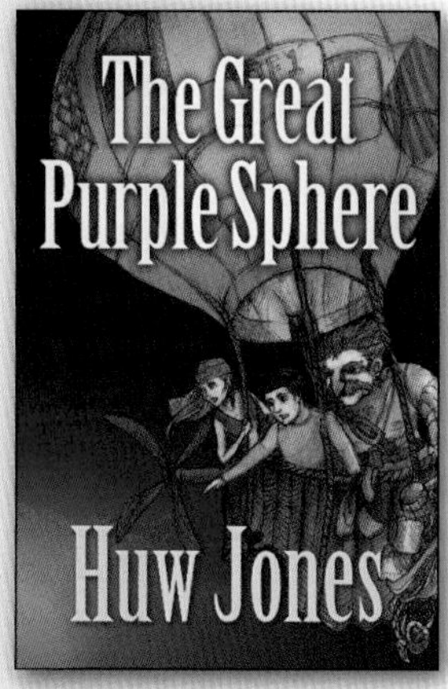

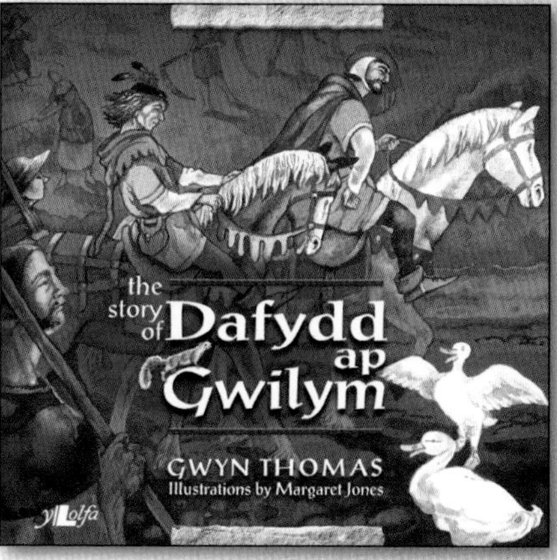